BLACKMANE'S CHEST

A REALMS OF GLOMORA SHORT

DAVID B. CORDER

To my wife, Abigail.
Without you, this book, and my life, would not be possible.
Tha gaul agam ort.

TABLE OF CONTENTS

CHAPTER ONE

"I'M LUCKY I even stumbled upon him, sir."

Veran Bloodstalker glanced from the farmer to the man in the back of the wagon. The fat, richly dressed man was clearly dying. Cuts decorated his body in numerous places across his torso, flesh lacerated as if it were a side of pork. One hand draped over the side of the wagon as the farmer continued in a hushed, hurried tone.

"There I was, headin' towards ma cousin's on the Storm Cloud Road through Tharsus woods, and I come upon all these bodies, lurkin' there in the dark. 'Sweet Sallee,' I said to myself. 'Look at them.' Dead, every single one of them. Their horses too. Then I looked in the carriage and nearly fainted. Blood. Blood was everywhere." The farmer paused and shook his head, looking a bit green in the weak moonlight. "It was the worst thing I ever did see."

Veran stood in silence, considering the farmer's words. He moved closer to the wagon, examining the gravely wounded man more closely. Moonlight glittered on the golden brooch at his neck, the visage of a black male lion encrusted in it. Veran considered the piece of jewelry for a moment.

A fine decoration. Yet whoever or whatever did this didn't take it.

He turned his full attention to the decimated form before him. "Who are you? Who did this to you?"

Blood bubbled at the man's lips as he tried to speak. He hacked and coughed weakly.

The farmer spoke from behind Veran. "He shouldn't

talk, sir. He hasn't got the strength."

"He's going to die," Veran said flatly. "He might as well tell me what did this so that he has a chance of being avenged."

The fat man gasped, though not from shock at Veran's words. His gaze fixed on Veran, and in those glassy eyes, recognition of the truth shone. He took a few shuddering breaths then spoke. "I…I am Lord Tav B-Blackmane…the p-phantom…it wiped out…"

Veran listened to the fat man's raspy, struggled words and then to his shallow, labored breathing. When Blackmane had finished sharing what he'd seen, his eyes dimmed to black stones, gleaming dully in the moonlight.

The farmer cleared his throat. "Oh, dear Sallee… He's done died." He positioned himself over the dead man and murmured what sounded like a prayer, clutching a pendant at his neck. When he'd finished, he turned to Veran. "What do we do now, sir?"

Veran pondered what the fat man had said. The man's words seemed unlikely—not impossible, true, but certainly improbable. If he were to unravel this enigma, he needed a second opinion. Perhaps this farmer could get him to the one place where he was likely to find a reliable second opinion on such an odd turn of events. He turned to the farmer. "What was your name again?"

"Squine, sir."

"Well, Squine, let's get a move on." Veran clambered up into the back of the wagon, careful not to step on its freshly acquired corpse. He sat on the edge near one of the wheels and looked down on the farmer. "To the tavern. I need a drink."

***

THE DARK FORM of The Ghostly Damsel hid within a cloak of gloomy trees just off the road. An owl called from the shadows as Squine drew his horse to a stop. Veran dropped from the wagon, making his way up to where Squine sat. "Are you sure you won't come in?" he asked.

The farmer shook his head. "No, sir, I will not. I'm movin' on to Draemar immediately and lettin' the guard know what happened. Besides, it wouldn't seem right, leavin' a dead body out in the cold while I'm enjoyin' ale. Such callous actions bring a man bad luck."

The dead man isn't going anywhere, but to each their own. Veran shrugged. "Suit yourself." He turned to head towards the tavern with windows that glowed like yellow cat eyes in the dark.

The farmer stopped him. "So, you're goin' to look into it? Into what killed the noble?"

Veran nodded. "I will." Blackmane's tale, being the puzzle that it was, had intrigued Veran greatly, and he wanted to get to the bottom of it. "Whatever killed him and his caravan will no doubt be a danger to others who pass through Tharsus Woods. Whatever is lurking there needs to be exterminated."

Squine was silent. His eyes drifted to the sword that rested on Veran's back. The farmer shifted in his seat and toyed with the reins as he stared at the weapon. ShadowWeep unsettled people. It was simple, yet elegant. In the center of its guard was the engraving of a black rose, and in the pommel glimmered two jewels: one black as night, the other a brilliant dark blue sapphire. No, it wasn't the sword's appearance. It was the *aura* that unnerved those who saw it.

"There's something wicked about that sword," Squine whispered.

Veran cracked a smile. The farmer didn't seem to have

meant for him to hear. "You have no idea."

Squine shook his head. "I'll let the guard in Draemar know I ran into you... It was Veran, correct?"

"Yes, but they know me better by Bloodstalker."

"Ah... Yes..."

"Just let them know that I'm looking into it. Tell them to meet me here as soon as possible. If I'm not here, then I'm in Tharsus Woods where the attack happened. Understand?"

"Yes, sir. Sallee's blessings upon you. Come on, Galbert." Squine gave another click of his tongue and urged his horse along.

As he passed, Veran gave a final glance at the dead man in his wagon, the blood on the pallid face like the splotches of some rancid disease in the moonlight. He turned away and headed to the tavern's door.

A cold autumn wind stirred Veran's hair as he pulled on the iron handle and stepped inside. He was greeted by the warm, crackling light of the fire in the hearth at the center of the room and the laughter and din of the patrons scattered at tables inside. An elf bard, her hair golden-red as a sunset, filled the tavern with a flute's lilting notes from a far corner.

The large man serving drinks behind the bar looked up as Veran approached. His gaze raked over Veran in quick assessment. "What can I do you for?" he asked.

"I'm looking for Ruald Firegem." Veran continued to scan the tavern. A few patrons' glances strayed his way, but they quickly returned to their drinks. The bartender nodded towards a staircase in the back corner of the tavern. "There's a table under those stairs that he likes to hole up in. Doesn't like to be bothered except on business."

A smile touched Veran's lips. His old friend hadn't changed a bit. "Oh, believe me, I'm aware. He'll be happy to see me." He headed towards the staircase. Under it, a dwarf sat at a table, a large battle-axe leaning on the wall next to him. On hand was a tankard that was, unsurprisingly, empty. The bald dwarf ran his fingers through his beard, which was such a bright red it was almost orange. He was squinting down at a piece of parchment in front of him. Veran grinned at the sight and then spoke up. "Don't stare at it too hard. I'd hate for the only dwarf in Zeral to have his head explode because he can't understand what he's reading."

Ruald jerked his head up, his eyes widening. "Veran! You sorry scoundrel! By the stone gods, it is you!"

Veran laughed as the dwarf got down from his chair and pulled him into a firm hug. "Come now, Ruald! You're embarrassing me. I don't want the ladies to get the wrong idea about us."

"Oh, dash it all, Veran. They can all see that I'm much too pretty for you."

Veran roared with laughter. He could always count on Ruald for a good joke.

"Come, sit down, I'll call for a meal. Sonja!"

A dark-haired beauty with soft eyes came over from the bar. "Yes, Ruald?"

"Get this man whatever he wants. My treat," he added with an assertive nod at Veran. "Also, it's a complete mystery to me, but it appears that all of my ale has vanished. Could I trouble you for another?"

She smiled. "Of course." She looked to Veran. "And what would you like?"

Veran removed his hood. He had no interest in conversing with his old friend from the shadows of a cowl. "Roasted chicken and potatoes. As for my drink, whatever he's having."

Sonja nodded, still smiling, and went to fetch their refreshments.

Veran nodded towards the parchment that Ruald had been reading. "Something vexing about that piece of parchment you were reading?"

Ruald rolled his eyes. "Some gabbing old woman left

it for me at the bar earlier this afternoon. It's a request to clear her garden of gargatoads. I don't have time for such nonsense, and she's not even close to paying my usual rate."

"It's good to see that the famous Firegem has not fallen to the dismal level of slaying enlarged amphibians." Ruald chuckled. "How long has it been? Two, three years?"

"Something like that. I was traveling down south through Mirvene and Vitar, doing what I do best."

"Causing trouble."

Veran smirked. "More or less."

"Well, it does my old heart good to see you again. A friendly face is hard to come by these days. Had occasion to slay any vampires recently or have you retired the name Bloodstalker? And how are Mirius and Teyla?"

"I haven't retired my hunt for bloodsuckers. I doubt if I ever will. If I do, it will be when I'm too old and weak to lift my sword." Veran shook his head. "As for Mirius and Teyla, I couldn't tell you. I haven't seen them in about seven months. We were near The Great Wood when we all separated. Mirius went into the forest to meet with the elf tribes of the hurúnae, and Teyla went with him."

"The parting was amicable I hope?" Ruald asked.

Veran scowled. Hardly. He and Teyla had fought. The female wizard was usually calm and serene, but the day that the three of them had separated, she had been angry, a mood that was frightening to behold when the woman could channel her fury into lightning bolts and orbs of flame. The two of them had been at each other's throats up until the moment she'd walked off with Mirius and had left him in the dust, frustrated and angry. "It could have been better," he admitted.

Sonja returned with their drinks. She gave Veran a shy smile as she placed his tankard before him.

He smiled back and watched her as she drifted over to another table.

Ruald smirked. "She's quite the beauty, eh?"

Veran smiled. "Quite." But she was no Teyla.

Ruald took his tankard and lifted it in the air. "A toast to you, Veran. One of the best men I have ever met."

"And to Ruald. The best bounty hunter I have ever met."

They tapped their drinks together and took long draughts. Veran liked the ale. It had a hint of something that gave it a pleasant flavor. Sweet, like cinnamon.

Ruald let out a belch and then cleared his throat. "So, why *are* you here?"

Veran grew serious. "Ever heard of Lord Tav Blackmane?"

"Should I have?"

"Doesn't really matter if you have. Poor man is dead. Just saw him pass on to the next world not an hour ago."

Ruald raised an eyebrow. "You didn't have anything to do with giving him passage, did you?"

Veran smirked. "Me? Come now, my dwarven friend. You know how fond I am of aristocrats."

Ruald stared at him flatly.

"No." He relented with a shake of his head. "It wasn't me who killed him."

"Well, then, what did? Don't keep me waiting for my hair to grow back!"

"A phantom."

An incredulous look passed over Ruald's face. "I think you ought to start from the beginning."

"Very well. I've been traveling north towards the Moon Court. I planned to stop here on my way up for old time's sake to see if you were around. A few miles from here, I caught the sound of wagon wheels clattering. Then I saw the light of a lantern bobbing about in the dark. It was heading towards me, so I stood aside to let the wagon pass. However, the wagon stopped in front of me, and its driver, a farmer named Squine, asked me if I was a healer. He had found a man gravely wounded on Storm Cloud

Road in Tharsus Woods along with a whole caravan.
According to Squine, he was the only survivor."
    "Your Blackmane, I presume?" Ruald asked.
    "You presume correctly. I said I couldn't heal him, but
I asked Blackmane, as hurt as he was, who had attacked
him. He was covered in cuts as if wounded by a sword."
    "So, some sort of assassin?" Ruald interrupted. "But
you just told me he was killed by a phantom."
    Veran shook his head. "That's what Blackmane told
me."
    A look of consternation came over the dwarf's face.
"Since when do phantoms leave blade marks?"
    "They don't. But Blackmane said something unseen
attacked him and his guards, and whatever it was showed
no mercy. I think it was a fluke that Blackmane survived
the attack. The description of the slaughter that Squine
gave was quite horrendous."
    "Did Blackmane say anything else?"
    Veran waved his hand. "Not as such no." He took a sip
of his ale. "He died right after he told me what had
attacked him. Or, at least, what he *thought* attacked him.
However, Squine told me that when he loaded Blackmane
into his wagon, he was mumbling something about a chest
being taken."
    "A chest, eh?" The dwarf's eyes gleamed with interest.
"What kind of chest?"
    "No idea. Squine said he found no chest in the
carriage or anywhere else among the carnage."
    "Our farmer friend could be a liar," Ruald pointed out.
    "He could be," Veran agreed. "But I didn't get that
sense about him. He wouldn't have mentioned the chest at
all if he had taken it for himself. I think the assassin took
Blackmane's chest, if indeed there was one."
    "Phantoms don't tend to go around taking chests."
    "No, they don't. More reason I believe Blackmane was
mistaken."
    "And you, Bloodstalker?" Ruald asked. "What do you

think?"

A mischievous grin spread across Veran's face. "I think I'm going to do some hunting."

Ruald smiled as he took a draught. He slammed the tankard on the table and wiped his mouth with the back of his hand. "I imagined so, but you still haven't told me what has brought you here when Tharsus Woods is in the other direction."

"I wanted to get your opinion on the matter. Squine has taken Blackmane's body to Draemar. It's implied that's where he and his caravan were heading, and being the rich noble that he is—sorry, was—the city is going to want to know about his death. I told Squine to have the guard send some troops to meet me here so that they can investigate. However, given the distance between here and Draemar, I don't imagine that they'll arrive until late morning. After all, it is past midnight as it is. In the meantime, I'll rise with the dawn and investigate the attack to see what I can find. If it is a phantom, I'd best do my inquiring and poking about in daylight."

"And what if it's not a phantom?"

"Well, that's why I have ShadowWeep." Veran flicked his finger against the hilt of his sword.

Ruald laughed. "And would you like me along? It's been some time since I gave Ergatha a good swing." He patted the battle-axe in question affectionately.

"Not this time my friend. I'd like you to stay here to be my liaison with the city guard. If I don't end up coming back, someone has to tell them my plan." He paused, noting the puckered frown on Ruald's face. "Now, don't go getting sour-faced on me. I also need someone to negotiate a bounty with them for the killing of this creature as well as a reward for returning the good Blackmane's stolen property."

"And I imagine"—Ruald cleared his throat—"that as the negotiator of this bounty, I would somehow be entitled to a percentage?"

Veran shrugged. "I'm sure you would. It's a lot of work to negotiate with the city guard."

"Isn't it now? You'd have an easier time ridding a werewolf of fleas. As for my opinion on the matter, I believe you're right. A phantom using a sword doesn't seem right. It's something else, and I agree that you should check into it. Storm Cloud is a frequently traveled road. Anyone who uses it could be in danger. But Veran?" The dwarf fixed him with his eyes. "You need to be careful."

"Aren't I always?"

"Not when we fought those harpies on that bridge." Veran laughed. "It wasn't that far of a drop."

"I suppose not, but it certainly established you as a reckless lunatic in my eyes from that point forward."

Veran chuckled as Sonja brought him his chicken and potatoes.

CHAPTER TWO

"WELL, YOU'RE A hungry lot." Veran watched the murder of crows picking at the remains of Blackmane's caravan.

He counted sixteen bodies scattered among the remains of a dead campfire and other camping paraphernalia. Eight of them were horses, six dressed in war gear, two harnessed to the carriage. The rest of the bodies belonged to Blackmane's bodyguards and his coachman. One guard slumped in the body of the carriage, his feet dangling out of the open door. A last defense for the cowering nobleman as the phantom culled its way through all of his guards?

Veran knelt to examine the nearest corpses. Cuts riddled their flesh in the same way they had riddled Blackmane's. There was no doubt in the Bloodstalker's mind that they were made by a sword. Not for the first time since the night before, Veran puzzled over how a phantom could have wreaked such carnage.

He approached the carriage where the guard inside was not only cut up but eviscerated, his blood and entrails splashed against the rich leather seats. Now Veran knew why Squine had been so horrified when recalling what he had seen. Veran might have been in the same state as the farmer at the sight if he had not seen bloodshed much worse in his lifetime.

What he saw solidified his doubts that it was a phantom. A phantom did not attack with such ferocity and rip apart its victims. If it were not for the sword cuts on the bodies, Veran would have thought that a raging bear had attacked the caravan. Still, nothing he saw answered his original question of where the caravan's attacker had gone. He would need more than the evidence he could see with mortal sight.

Veran closed his eyes. Reaching deep inside himself, he muttered under his breath. *"Mi varte nu gaul."* When he opened his eyes, his senses were ten times more vivid. He could see in shades that his normal eyes could not behold, see the outlines of small creatures even when hidden by forest, and he was able to perceive the world in both its fullness and its nuance. Perhaps ordinary sight couldn't tell him where the attacker had gone, but with this, he could track whoever was responsible with ease.

The scent of blood was intoxicating. The carriage reeked with the rusty aroma, and it brought back memories, memories that made his mouth water. He tried to shake off the desire to drink buckets full of the stuff, to rip into anyone foolish enough to pass by him without realizing who he was, *what* he was. He thought about Ruald, sitting in The Ghostly Damsel. The pretty girl, Sonja. Squine the farmer. The elf bard. He could kill them all and drink every drop from their body. He could assault Draemar and slaughter every human there and have a feast worthy of all the vampires in Glomora.

We can kill them all, Veran, a voice spoke from deep within his mind. *Kill them, and drink them dry.*

"Yes," Veran whispered. "Yes, we could."

Just as he decided to turn back and head towards The Ghostly Damsel to slay its inhabitants, he froze in his tracks. A glint of consciousness broke through the gluttonous haze, and the dim echo of a female voice resounded in his mind.

Control it.

Veran came back to himself, gritting his teeth. The intense thirst passed as he took control of ShadowWeep's magic. It had been so long since he had used this power that he had forgotten how even just a little bit could overwhelm him. He had to do better.

Breathing in deeply, Veran took in the scent of blood around him. He let it fill his being until he was as familiar with it as he would be with a lover. Faint traces of the scent were on the air, leading from the road deeper into the woods.

Veran followed it, passing into the trees. He left behind the potent aroma where large pools of blood had been spilled, following the smallest hints of it into the forest. But as he continued forward and the smell behind him grew fainter, the traces he was tracking grew more pronounced.

Half an hour passed. The scent of blood continued to grow until it was overwhelmingly potent. Then he heard the sound of rushing water. Pushing through the trees, Veran found himself at the edge of a cliff overlooking a small vale. A waterfall cascaded from the cliffside opposite him, crashing down in violent white to fill a pool about fifty feet below.

The smell of the blood was at its strongest here. Behind the waterfall, in the side of the cliff, was the edge of a hollow opening. The opening to a cave? Had he found the dwelling of Blackmane's so-called phantom?

A copse of birch trees waved in the wind next to the edge of the pool, and Veran focused on them with his improved vision. He could see someone standing there—a slim man dressed in leather armor with shoulder-length black hair and a sword on his hip.

Veran crouched and backed away from the edge just enough to be inconspicuous. The man below was not a phantom, and Veran knew that he was not the one who had attacked Blackmane. Though the scent of his blood was deliciously palpable, he wasn't the source of the blood aroma that Veran had tracked through the trees. He was, however, near it.

The man had to be some sort of lookout, which confirmed Veran's suspicion that there was a cave obscured by the waterfall. However, his distance from the cave and the cacophony of the raging water made it impossible for him to sense everything that was inside it. The scent of blood was the only thing his heightened senses could pick out.

But why would a phantom need a lookout? Were there more of them, or was there only one lookout keeping watch? With that sudden thought, Veran cursed himself and scanned the area around him. He should have looked around sooner. For all he knew, there was a marksman in the trees aiming an arrow at his heart.

His vision caught the outlines of birds and squirrels in the foliage. The pungent scent of their blood, not sweet like the blood of humans, tickled his nose. A deer grazed among the trees in some grass about fifteen yards away, a dark silhouette in the sunlight. The scent of its blood was odd and possessed a hint of some peculiar smell. He frowned and focused on it for a moment. It smelled wrong, but most likely, it merely carried some sort of disease, and Veran dismissed it. Finished scanning his surroundings, Veran returned his attention to the lookout.

It would have come in handy to be a better archer right

then, but as Mirius had once pointed out, Veran couldn't shoot the rear end of a troll. He would have to get in close and cut the man's throat quietly. There was a steep slope leading down the cliff into the trees below. He just had to be stealthy about getting down there.

Just as he shifted to move out, a cold tingle shot up Veran's spine. He looked around. Something had changed, but what?

His eyes roved the trees as he tried to deduce what had caused the disturbance. The deer. It was gone. He had not heard it move, even with his heightened senses. There was no trace of it, and no deer moved that quickly or quietly. In place of the deer's scent, there was a stench: the pure, ghastly aroma of únae blood.

Something sliced the air. Veran's eyes flickered to see a thin blur rushing at him, quick as a sparrow. He gawked, falling to his belly. A knife flew above his head and sank into a tree behind him with a *thunk*.

Veran scrambled to his feet, breaking the focus of his spell. His senses returned to normal as he drew ShadowWeep just in time to knock a second knife from the air. His hair fell into his eyes as he took a defensive pose, ready for a third should it come.

A woman stood before him. Her ears were pointed, and she had a mass of braided red hair. She wore a dress of soft deerskin, and her face was covered in the war paint of one of the hurúnae tribes of The Great Wood.

No wonder the deer had smelled odd. It hadn't had a disease. It had been the elf girl magically disguised but unable to completely cover the elf scent of her blood.

"Clever having a lookout that blends in so well with the scenery," Veran said. "But what if a hunter mistook you for an actual deer? I imagine that they would be disappointed when they saw that their kill had transformed back into a meek elf girl."

She drew a dagger in each hand, holding them up in a guarded stance. "You're not welcome here, bounty hunter."

"Really? What if I told you I brought pie?"

She dove at him with speed much greater than his own. Her daggers came up, and Veran blocked with his blade. The daggers glanced off, and as Veran swung ShadowWeep at her midsection she leaped back, his sword cutting through empty air.

The elf landed lightly on her feet then shot forward with another assault, stabbing her dagger at Veran's belly. He blocked it before she could reach his midsection, but as he did so, her second dagger struck at his face.

He leaned his head out of the way, but not fast enough. The dagger sliced across his cheek in a searing line of fire.

Grunting, Veran rammed his shoulder into her chest, knocking the wind from her and sending her back. He brought his sword over his head in a downward strike that would have cleaved her in two had she not twisted out of the way. With his guard down, the elf took advantage of the opening and plunged both her daggers into his torso.

Veran gasped, stumbling backward, her weapons protruding from his chest. She's too agile. Both daggers had missed his heart, but the sharp, throbbing pain was excruciating.

Another knife appeared in his adversary's hand, her eyes glimmering with the thrill of the potential kill. She jumped, spinning in mid-air to deliver the final strike.

A sudden rush of magic tore through his soul as a word of power escaped his lips. "*Torja!*"

The girl was blocked by an invisible wall. She yelped as it shoved her backward and over the side of the cliff.

Veran gritted his teeth and removed the daggers from his chest, sending them clattering to the ground. Blood stained his leather tunic, and he gave a sheepish shake of his head. He hadn't been expecting a bandit so skilled.

He heard the snapping of twigs behind him and turned to see the first lookout from before rushing out of the trees, his sword drawn. Veran cursed his luck as he raised his sword despite the stabbing pain in his chest. The two men's blades clashed and locked.

The bandit grinned. "Looks like you tangled with Hina. You ain't goin' to live much longer."

The toe of his boot collided with Veran's shin, sending a sharp pain up the vampire hunter's leg as he collapsed, grunting. ShadowWeep flew from his grasp as the bandit gave a violent swing of his sword. Then he cut across Veran's side, sending up a shower of blood.

Veran let out a sharp scream as a shower of red flashed before his eyes. Desperately he clawed for his inner magic, but it eluded him. A cold, confused panic washed over him as he collapsed. Why couldn't he sense his magic?

He gazed up at the bandit, his gloating face going in and out of focus. Then he remembered the bandit's words.

The elf. Her daggers must have been laced with some sort of toxin.

The bandit smirked as he looked down on Veran. The sound of shifting rocks and dirt came from the cliff's edge.

"Hina, are you alright?" the bandit called.

"Fine, Bran." The elf lifted herself over the lip of the cliff. She was bruised and scraped, but alive. "He almost had me. I didn't think he could do magic. It took a minute, but now the venom is doing its trick."

Bran looked back at Veran. "What should we do with him? She will probably want to know how he found us. And there might be more bounty hunters."

She?

"We best be quick," Hina said. "The adder venom and all that blood loss will kill him within the next few minutes."

Bran nodded and grabbed a handful of Veran's hair, lifting his head. "How did you find us, troll fungus?"

Despite himself, Veran grinned. "Oh, that's easy, I just followed the scent of cow dung. Your breath reeks of it."

If he was about to die, he was certainly going to have some fun while doing it.

Bran scowled. He pushed Veran's face into the dirt and dug his knee into his bloody side causing Veran to cry out. "How. Did. You. Find. Us?"

"Go to hell," Veran hissed through clenched teeth.

"You first." The bandit stood, ready to bring his sword down for the final stroke.

Veran braced himself.

An arrow sank into the bandit.

The man looked at the arrow protruding from his chest in disbelief, wavered, and then fell to the ground. Looking for the source of the arrow, Hina drew a knife only to have a second arrow catch her between the eyes. She went spinning off the cliff with a short, clipped scream, and after a couple of heartbeats, a large splash followed. She wasn't climbing back up again.

Veran blinked, shocked at his good luck. The arrow sticking out of the bandit was fletched in familiar dark purple feathers.

The bushes rustled nearby, and then footsteps drew closer. "Having some trouble, Veran?"

Veran struggled to look up, weak as he was. Standing over him was a familiar face.

"Mirius."

CHAPTER THREE

THE DARK ELF grinned at Veran, his bow in hand, the sun glinting off his snow-white hair. "It's been a long time, Veran. Nine months since we parted at the edge of The Great Wood?"

"It hasn't been that long." Veran forced himself to a sitting position, his wounds screeching in protest. "I'm pretty sure it's only been seven."

"Has it?" Mirius kneeled next to Veran. "You're pretty cut up." He glanced warily about him. "I don't think we're going to have any more company—at least for now. We need to get you healed."

Veran nodded. "If there are more bandits, they're in a cave behind the waterfall. They probably didn't hear our tussle out here. Just give me a minute. Let me concentrate." He closed his eyes.

His world was swimming, the venom blurring and distorting his senses. He did his best to focus, to manifest the power that rested within. Then he began chanting under his breath. "*Naivya, paran tan mi vi...Naivya, paran tan mi vi...*"

A warm glow began to swell in his core, spreading throughout his body. The disorientation brought on by the venom faded, and the places where he had been cut knitted back together into scarless flesh. After a few seconds, all the pain ebbed away, leaving him whole again. Veran opened his eyes to see Mirius staring at him.

The dark elf wrinkled his nose. "It's always so gross to watch that."

"Then don't watch. Now, what are you doing here?"

Mirius opened his mouth to answer, but another

familiar voice interrupted him. "Looking for you, obviously."

Veran's heart dropped. A slender woman dressed in blue robes slipped out of the brush Mirius had just come through. Her sun-gold hair hung to her shoulders, and her eyes fixed on Veran with an unnerving gaze.

"Teyla."

"Slowpoke." Mirius's gaze danced mischievously to the wizard then back to Veran.

She smiled that same smile that always left the vampire hunter confused and infatuated. He was lost in her crystal blue eyes as if he were a bird wandering a clear, endless sky. Those eyes were always able to see into the deepest reaches of Veran's soul, into depths he did not want anyone to fathom. The wizard peering into the most fragile and darkest corners of his being had been a point of contention between the two of them for as long as they had known each other. Given the nature of their last meeting, he especially did not want Teyla to see into his soul now and perceive how convoluted his feelings for her had become.

"I thought you'd be happier to see me, Veran."

Veran lowered his gaze. "I am as pleased as a sailor who has spotted a siren. But why are the two of you looking for me? And how did you find me?"

"The answer to the second question is that we found Ruald at The Ghostly Damsel after Teyla teleported us. He told us you were on a job. We found Blackmane's carriage and tracked you the rest of the way." A smug smile planted itself on Mirius's face.

Veran gave him an incredulous look. "You tracked me? Since when are you able to track me, Mirius?"

A wicked glimmer passed through Mirius's eyes. The shadúnae's smile grew wider. "I picked up a lot of tricks during my time with the hurúnae. You're not as elusive as you think, Bloodstalker."

Veran smiled. "Very well. But why were you looking for me?"

"That can wait," Teyla said. "We need to tend to your wounds."

Veran blinked. "I've already healed myself. This is just blood."

Teyla's face went stony, her mouth tightening into a thin line. "You're still using that magic, then."

Veran returned her fierce stare. *She's still on about this, huh? Even after all this time.* "I am." He stood and collected ShadowWeep, sheathing it on his back. "It's my power to use."

Teyla opened her mouth to say something, but then she clamped it shut. She moved past Veran to the cliff's edge and looked down into the vale. "So, were these the only two bandits you had to kill, Veran?"

Veran knew he hadn't heard the last of her thoughts on his magic. He walked over and stood beside her. "I don't know. I don't imagine so, and even if they were, there's still this 'phantom' to deal with, whatever it may be."

"For the record," Mirius said, "I'm the one who killed the bandits. Just in case we're keeping score."

Teyla ignored the elf. "Yes, Ruald told us about this phantom. It's quite a puzzle."

"One of the bandits was a wild elf. Before she attacked me, she was magically disguised as a deer. It's possible she also used magic to become invisible when attacking the Blackmane carriage. Perhaps she was the phantom?"

Mirius shook his head. "Doubtful. Many hurúnae are blessed with the ability to shapeshift, but I've never heard of them having the ability to turn invisible unless she possessed other magic."

"If she had had other magic, she wouldn't have fought me with knives," Veran said. "And I doubt you would have struck her down with an arrow so easily. So, the phantom is still about somewhere. Probably in that cave behind the waterfall." He pointed out the hint of the cave opening just at the edge of the falling water. "And who knows how many more bandits are in there."

Teyla nodded. "Well, I will take a look." She closed her eyes and started speaking in the language of the Old Magic.

Her form changed as she shrank, her hair and skin morphing into feathers, her feet elongating and sprouting tiny talons. Within moments, the wizard had become a small blue bird. The bird gave a blink of its beady eyes and flew off, flitting to the waterfall below.

Mirius and Veran watched for a few moments.

Finally, the dark elf broke the silence. "So, you two still have a lot of tension, eh?"

"Shut up, Mirius."

"Yes, your lordship. However, you know the two of you will need to talk about it eventually."

"Eventually. When will you tell me why you two were looking for me?"

Mirius shook his head. "Now's not the time. It can wait. We'll discuss it when we finish the job before us, just like old times. Ruald mentioned that there might be some coin involved."

Veran scoffed. "You're probably thinking you'll be

entitled to some of the reward."

"Do dragons covet gold?"

"Yes, and, apparently, so do greedy elves."

Mirius's yellow eyes gleamed. "I'm not greedy. I just look for opportunity."

Veran shook his head, biting back a smile.

A few minutes went by as the two of them listened to the crashing of the waterfall. Veran caught the flitting form of Teyla as she flew back to them, shooting across the smooth surface of the pool and ascending on the air up the cliff face. She landed next to them and reverted to her human form. She knelt on the grass, her hair covering her face.

"There's four more in there," she said. "Though one of them irks me more than the rest."

"Why is that?" Veran asked.

"She's a vampire," she said, her voice grim.

Veran looked at her sharply. "Are you sure?"

She nodded. "Her eyes were black, and she had fangs."

It explained the overwhelming smell of blood that led Veran from the road to this place and why that guard had been torn to pieces. The poor man had been dined on by the vampire, and his blood no doubt had soaked into the vampire's clothes.

"Why would everyday bandits side with a vampire?" Mirius frowned. "Shouldn't they be fodder for her?"

"Typically, yes, but the fact that they seem to all be on the same side does not bode well. Unless the bandits are not aware of her true identity, which I doubt. She is our phantom, I'm sure, and she used some sort of arcanist invention or spell to make herself invisible when she attacked the caravan." Veran stood and thought. "She also made off with Blackmane's chest, and that disturbs me. Vampires seldom turn to mere thievery, and she left his golden brooch on his person. She's not interested in mere treasure. Something powerful is in that chest, I guarantee you, and she's probably promising the bandits payment for their help. After all, it never hurts to have a few thugs around to watch your back and guard you while you sleep."

"Yet she wiped out that entire caravan presumably by herself?" Teyla asked. "From what Ruald told us, there were no words about bandits attacking the caravan."

Veran nodded. "I'm sure that she was the only one who attacked, and she enjoyed doing it too. She even killed the horses in her course of bloodletting."

"So, what should we do?" Mirius asked.

Veran launched into a plan, the gears in his mind turning rapidly. "We need to draw the rest of the bandits out. A black-eyed vampire means she's young, and she won't be able to survive in the sunlight, so if we can take them down first, then we can get to her. You two let me handle her. Mirius, I want you to position yourself here. Cloak yourself in the trees, and as the bandits emerge from the cave, take them down with your arrows. I'll engage them in melee if it comes to it. Once all of them have been taken out, I can move in and kill the vampire." He looked at Teyla. "I'll need a distraction to extract the worms from the dirt, Lady Bluewing."

Teyla smiled. "I thought you'd never ask. I have something chilling in mind."

Veran smiled at her for the first time since she'd shown up. "I can't wait to see what you have in store."

CHAPTER FOUR

VERAN MADE HIS way down the slope to the collection of trees where he had spotted the first lookout. The water was louder here. As he edged closer to the pool, he spotted Hina's corpse floating in the water, Mirius's arrow sticking up like a tower from her brow. It was a good thing that his friends had arrived. If they hadn't, it might have been his body bobbing about in the pool.

He emerged from the trees and stopped about ten yards away from where the water crashed into the pool. Here, he could see the entirety of the entrance to the cave, its yawning blackness stretching open like the maw of some monstrous creature. He drew ShadowWeep, its keening song emitting from its blade as he pulled it from its scabbard.

He waited. Gradually, the air became colder, and there was a soft cracking. Veran turned to see the pool freezing over rapidly, gray-white ice spreading over it in a wave. Hina's corpse was frozen into place, one hand reaching up as if begging someone to pull her up from the terrible cold. Soon the entire pool was frozen solid, and the arcane wave of ice was creeping up the waterfall, crystalizing it from the bottom to the top. Within seconds, Veran was staring at a pillar of ice that stretched up the cliff face. The cracking stopped, and all was still. Mirius hadn't been the only one who had learned a few things during Veran's absence.

A few moments went by before Veran heard the echoing of voices coming from inside the cave. They were incoherent, but he could sense their confusion and bewilderment, most likely wondering why the sound of the waterfall had suddenly stopped. They were probably also wondering why it had become cold so suddenly. Veran watched as three bandits emerged from the cave, gawking with their faces turned upward as they looked at the huge pillar of ice. They looked at one another in dumb silence, weapons dangling from their fingers. Then they saw Veran.

"Good morning, lads! Fine day, isn't it?" Veran flashed a smile, resting ShadowWeep on his shoulder. "Bit chilly though, if I do say so."

"Sorcerer!" A bandit with a large nose charged at Veran, the other two following his lead.

The air shrieked as arrows fell from the sky and found their marks. The two bandits in the back fell dead, and as the big-nosed one turned to look at his fallen comrades, an arrow pierced his heart, sending him to the ground. Veran held up a hand in gratitude to Mirius, knowing that, wherever the shadúnae was hiding, he could see it.

Veran stalked towards the cave. The vampire would be alert, waiting for him. He mentally ran through how he would move about within the cave when he stopped in his tracks.

Someone was emerging from the darkness. She wore a dark cloak over a shirt of chainmail and held a sword, her black bangs hanging in her eyes. Her bloodlust was palpable, and a dark aura stirred around her that resonated with the magic that was in Veran's sword.

It was the vampire that Teyla had spoken of, but something was wrong. She couldn't have been more than a century old and was certainly not old enough to withstand the sun's rays. There was something amiss.

As Veran held up a hand and made a sign for Mirius not to fire at her, he spotted the glint of silver on her finger. She wore a ring with a black stone set in it.

"Ah, so now I know where the 'phantom' came from. That ring also explains why you can stand in the light." Veran rubbed the stubble on his face in thought. "This is going to be interesting."

The she-vampire stared at Veran. "You're the Bloodstalker. I recognize that sword you carry. You're quite the legend. Although, I did not expect you were capable of something like this." She nodded toward the pillar of ice that loomed over them like a frosty giant.

Veran smirked. "Sorry, I can't take credit for that. I have friends in hiding. You're impossibly outnumbered, and it would be best for you to surrender now."

Her eyes widened. Then a laugh escaped from her mouth. She held the back of her hand to her lips, stifling giggles. "You're funny, Bloodstalker. Tell me, have you ever known a vampire to surrender willingly?"

"I have."

She flashed her fangs in a sardonic smile. "Is it because of the mercy you offer them? I've heard that before you kill a vampire, you offer them a chance at redemption. You claim you have a cure that can turn them human again. In fact, I heard that you were once a vampire yourself, serving under Varl of Crimsonfall. Tell me, is there any truth to any of that gibberish?"

"It's all true," Veran said. "I did not expect to meet a vampire here, but now that I have, I will offer you the same mercy." He reached into his tunic and pulled out a small glass vial. Inside was a dark red liquid that swished about. "If you drink this blood, you can have the vampire curse lifted from you. You can be human again, and you can start fresh. You are not that old. I can tell from your eyes. You can have the chance to redeem yourself before you suffer centuries of evil and wanton abandon. Trust me, it is not a fate that you wish to have."

He saw the glimmer of interest in her eyes. Part of him would sooner kill her given the slaughter she had brought upon Blackmane and his guards. Who knew how many other people she had killed? Instead, he struggled to put his selfishness and pride aside. He had made a promise to offer every vampire he encountered the same mercy that was once given to him if he was able. He would only impose justice if mercy was rejected.

The glimmer flickered and went out, and the vampire cackled as she raised her sword. "You are a damned fool, Veran Bloodstalker. I will not surrender my immortality as you have. Before you die, know that it was Gaika of Spiderhollow who put an end to your idiocy."

She vanished into thin air.

Veran tightened his grip on his sword and listened. There was not a sound. Even the wind was dead. He knew all too well the speed and stealth of a vampire. If he was not careful, then he would be skewered before he knew it.

Veran gasped as he felt the cold, sharp point of steel graze his back. He leaped away just in time, twisting in midair and lashing out with ShadowWeep. There were sparks as his sword met metal, but he had not struck flesh.

Out of the corner of his eye, he saw a patch of grass stir. He turned and brought up his sword to guard. The vampire's unseen weapon crashed into his, their blades locking against one another. The air before him stirred, and the faint outline of the vampire moved. He blinked.

Was his imagination playing tricks on him?

The pressure against his sword changed, and Gaika's sword slid around the edge of his own. He cried out as the blade sank into his shoulder, the point scraping against bone. As quick as a wasp, Gaika yanked the sword out and thrust it into his left thigh. Veran stumbled with a curse, falling to his knee, his shoulder and thigh burning with agony. Bloodlust radiated off her, and he shivered at her desire for his death.

A sharp whistling sound pierced the air. Ice crystals as sharp as daggers exploded against the invisible vampire, sending ice and droplets of black blood flying. A loud scream assaulted Veran's eardrums.

Teyla has lucky aim. And thank the gods that she did. Regaining his footing, Veran brought ShadowWeep up in a deadly arc, aiming where Teyla's spell had hit. He felt it bite through chainmail, the sword's sharp edge ripping into Gaika's flesh.

There was another bloodcurdling scream as a female voice, clear as a bell, resonated in his mind. *Her head, Veran. Find her head.* Black liquid oozed from a point in space before him. He tossed a prayer to the gods and swung his sword just above where the blood ran.

There was the utterance of a caught breath and the sound of something wet tearing. Gaika's head suddenly appeared, rolling across the blood-stained grass. There was the quick clatter of metal as her sword appeared out of thin air and the thump of her invisible body as it crumpled to the ground.

Veran breathed a sigh of relief. He looked down at shocked, black eyes and the hint of fangs protruding from blood-stained lips. Bile rose in the back of his throat, the spark of a deep, old hatred igniting in his gut. It raged in his belly and mingled with a sudden wave of remorse. He shut his eyes against the tide of overpowering emotion that filled his heart.

You did what you had to, the voice whispered, as gentle as a wife's hand of comfort on her husband's shoulder.

Veran looked again at Gaika's head. "I offered you mercy, but now all that's left is justice." He sheathed his sword.

In the grass, he spotted the vial he had held earlier. He hadn't even realized that he had flung it away when the fight had started. He walked over and picked it up, and shoved it back into his tunic. He stared at the ground for a moment, numb to the pain of his wounds.

"Only justice," he whispered.

CHAPTER FIVE

THE MAGICAL COLD that Teyla had wrought on the waterfall and pool dispelled. Once again water cascaded into the lagoon in a roar of tumultuous, violent white. Teyla and Mirius came down from the cliff as Veran removed the shade ring from the vampire's hand. It took some feeling about, but after a few seconds, he had found it and slipped it off her finger. The rest of her corpse appeared as soon as it slipped off. He held the ring before him, admiring its craftsmanship.

"That's a shade ring." Teyla approached, her gaze falling on the object in Veran's hand. "I've heard of them, but I've never seen one before."

"What does it do?" Mirius asked.

"Shade rings turn the wearer invisible when they desire," Veran said. "For vampires, they have a secondary effect. Protection from the sun. Whatever arcanist made this had quite the skill."

Mirius toyed with the string on his bow. "I did not know such a device existed. Well, now we know why Blackmane thought it was a phantom that attacked him." He scoffed. "A phantom, indeed!"

Veran pocketed the ring. "And now she's dead, but we still have a chest to collect." He tried to stand, but a dizziness took over, and he tumbled onto his rear. He hissed in pain as he finally acknowledged his injuries.

Teyla shook her head. "You've done enough, and you're badly wounded. Let Mirius take care of it."

"I can heal myself in a few seconds," Veran said.

Teyla's eyes flashed like blue fires. "No."

Veran and Teyla glared at one another.

Mirius glanced nervously between the two of them and cleared his throat. "Let me have some fun, Ver. I can handle it."

Teyla held Veran's eyes for a few more seconds before he sighed. "Fine. Just be careful, and don't get killed. They may have set traps."

"I don't plan on it," the elf said. "I still have to spend all that bounty money that we're going to get." He moved towards the cave and disappeared into its maw, the darkness swallowing him whole.

"Take off your tunic." Teyla's usual gentle voice held a firmness Veran had all but forgotten.

He rolled his eyes but obeyed, taking off his tunic so she could heal his wounds. "I think I'm going to have to buy new clothes with some of that bounty money," Veran mused. "It appears that these are filled with holes."

"Hmph." Teyla knelt next to him, placed two fingers on the puncture wound in his left thigh, and closed her eyes. "*Paran den noa, para ni hava.*" Her fingers glowed with a soft blue-white light.

Veran tensed his muscles and sucked in a breath as a jolt of pain passed through his leg. The pain passed as quickly as it had come, and he relaxed. The wound closed, leaving no scar.

As Teyla moved to his shoulder, he looked at her. Not for the first time, her beauty left him stricken. Everything about her mesmerized him from the curve of her jaw and chin to the fullness of her lips. She repeated the same words of the Old Magic for the healing spell, the soft cadence of her voice sending shivers through his body. Her fingers continued to glow.

"You are still so worried about my use of magic,"

Veran said.

Teyla held her fingers over his shoulder, watching the wound left by the vampire's sword close. "I told you, Veran. There's something not right about it. It's costing you something."

"Yet you can't tell me what."

She bit her lip. "You're right. I can't. But I sense it, and it has something to do with Naivya and Voldrid."

At the mention of those two names, Veran could feel something like an itch at the back of his mind, as if two ghosts were knocking at the windows of his consciousness. ShadowWeep rested in the grass next to him, and it seemed as if both its jewels glimmered in response to Teyla's words.

"We've been over this, Teyla. I know that. They are the source of my magic. We can't all be a gifted wizard like you."

Teyla opened her mouth to protest.

He cut her off with a shake of his head. "I think now is a good time for you to tell me why you and Mirius were looking for me."

Finished healing his shoulder, Teyla looked at him.

He lowered his eyes just the tiniest fraction. He did not want her peering into his soul.

"I've been having visions," Teyla said. "For the first time in years."

"Visions of what?" Veran asked.

"Us," she said.

At the mention of that word, Veran's cheeks warmed.

She continued. "You, me, Mirius, and Ruald. And there have been others. Faces I don't recognize, all mixing together like a rainbow of paints in water.

Fighting, running, talking. I think something is going to happen soon. Something big."

"So that's why you found me? To bring these visions to pass?"

Teyla shook her head. "It's not exactly that. I think whatever is going to happen is going to happen soon, and when it does, we will all want to be together. As the Ancients say, two heads are better than one." She gave a wry smile. "Well, in this case, four."

Veran smirked. "Well, one of those heads is a little closer to the ground than the rest."

"That reminds me. Ruald was very angry that he was left behind. He told us to tell you that he had never been so insulted in his life."

Veran rolled his eyes. "That grumpy old dotard."

Teyla laughed. She took his hand, entwining her fingers in his. "I've missed you."

Veran looked at her. Old, deep feelings bubbled their way to the surface, feelings that he had struggled for the past seven months to bury, feelings that he distracted himself from by hunting vampires and a menagerie of other monsters. But in the quiet hours of the night, as sleep eluded him, Teyla's face would enter his dreams and haunt him. "I've missed you as well, Teyla."

Her lips parted as if she were about to say something when Mirius's voice cut her off.

"No sign of any more bandits." Mirius emerged from the mouth of the cave, toting something under his right arm against his ribs.

Veran's eyes widened. "The chest!"

Mirius snuck the object behind his back. "Oh, no you don't, Veran. This is mine. Finders' keepers and such."

Teyla rolled her eyes. "You're incorrigible, Mirius."

"And you're a nag," he replied deftly.

The wizard narrowed her eyes, and Veran stifled a laugh. Mirius wasn't wrong. However, he agreed with Teyla. "Mirius, that belongs to Blackmane." He pulled his tunic back on. "It's going to the guard."

"Oh, come on Ver. Can't we at least see what's inside?" He gave the chest a rattle, and something solid rolled around. "I bet it's a sapphire as large as a grapefruit."

Veran thought about it and shrugged. "Can't do any harm. But I get to open it."

Mirius sighed. "Fine. Let's just get to it." He lowered it to the ground.

Veran strode up to it, and as he did so, he felt a clawed, burning hand scratching at the back of his consciousness. With it came dark whispers and an ice-cold foreboding that dripped down his spine.

Vol, tote, nuin mar. Vol, tote, nuin mar.

The words repeated rapidly within his mind as he approached the chest. There was evidence that there had been a lock, now broken off. He got on his knees and lifted the lid.

The whispers ceased.

"Veran…" Teyla whispered. "What is it?"

He looked at her over his shoulder.

"A lot of trouble."

CHAPTER SIX

RUALD WAS AT a different table than the one he and Veran had sat at the previous evening. Seated with him were three men wearing chainmail. The white tunics they wore over the chainmail were stitched with a golden eagle, the symbol of the nation of Zeral. It looked as if Squine had accomplished his mission.

Veran recognized one of the guards as Parner Girda, one of Draemar's lieutenants. He had a thin black beard and sharp gray eyes. Veran had crossed paths with Parner on several occasions, including one incident where he'd had to rescue the guard from the jaws of a rather ornery werewolf.

Ruald grinned at the sight of Veran, Mirius, and Teyla as they approached, Veran holding Blackmane's chest under his arm. "Ah, I see our heroes return. Veran, I don't appreciate you leaving me behind while you went on your adventure, but I suppose I can forgive you. These fine gentlemen are from Draemar, and we were just negotiating the bounty for this phantom. I'm assuming you took care of it?"

Mirius answered for Veran. "We'll have to negotiate for a higher bounty than whatever you came up with, Ruald. There were five bandits involved, along with this phantom that attacked Blackmane, who turned out to be a bloodsucking wench."

Parner squinted at the dark elf. "'A bloodsucking wench'?"

"A vampire," Veran said. "Using a shade ring to move about in daylight and to turn herself invisible. That's what killed Blackmane."

The lieutenant stared at him. "Do you have proof?"

Veran sat the chest on the table. He opened it to show Gaika's severed head, her black eyes piercing even in death. Just at that moment, Sonja passed by the table and saw the head. She gave a high-pitched scream, dropping her collection of frothing tankards. There was an uproar from the other patrons as they drew their weapons, their eyes locked on Veran.

After the patrons of The Ghostly Damsel were calmed down by the reassurances of Ruald, the tavern's elven bard brought Sonja to the corner of the tavern and tried to soothe her with tea and gentle words. Parner shut the chest and drummed his fingers on its lid in thought.

Teyla elbowed Veran. "You have quite the way with women."

Veran did not reply, his ears pink.

"Well, it's no doubt you did a service for us once again, Veran Bloodstalker." Parner nodded at Teyla and Mirius. "As did your companions. I will arrange for some men to collect the bodies of Blackmane's caravan, as well as investigate the bandits' hideout. When all is said and done, I imagine you all will be awarded about two thousand Suns."

Veran glanced at Mirius, who looked as though he was about to faint from pure happiness as his eyes gleamed with the luster of two golden coins.

"We will gladly accept the sum," Veran said.

Parner nodded, his fingers continuing their rhythmic movement on the chest. "I do find it interesting that you found this chest. It has Blackmane's lion seal on it. No doubt it came from the noble's personal carriage when the vampire attacked. But you say it was empty?"

"As empty as a miser's heart," Mirius chirped.

Veran resisted the urge to roll his eyes. "There was nothing in it," he said. "There may have been coins or jewels or some other treasure that the bandits already spent or hidden away. My guess is it was hidden, given that they would have only acquired it last night. However, it was quite convenient that it was empty, otherwise we would not have been able to carry that severed head back here in such a lavish fashion."

Parner bit his lip. He stared at Veran for a long moment until his fingers finally ceased their drumming. Then he nodded and stood, pushing the chest across the wooden table to one of his guards with an irritating scraping sound.

"We will be back in two days with your reward. We will have to speak to our superiors in Draemar, but there shouldn't be any trouble given your reputation, Bloodstalker." He nodded at Ruald, Mirius, and Teyla. "A good day to you all, and once again, thank you for your help." He looked at his guards and jerked his head at the door. "Let's go."

Veran watched them navigate through the maze of tables to the tavern door. Parner cast one last look over his shoulder at the vampire hunter. Veran saw suspicion in his eyes, and he returned the look with a stony expression. Parner turned and followed the other guards out, shutting the door behind him.

Ruald lowered his voice. "What was all of that about?"

Veran shook his head vehemently. "Later. For now, I am hungry and thirsty. Now is the time for food and drink."

Mirius sighed wistfully. "I think I'm too excited about the promise of all that coin to eat. Ruald, I have to thank you. I don't think we could have gotten that much money if we'd negotiated on our own."

The dwarf shrugged. "Well, I am getting a percentage. A man tends to work harder if he himself is gaining something from it. Don't think it had anything to do with you lot."

Mirius laughed, and he and the dwarf fell into reminiscing. As they talked, Veran felt Teyla's eyes on him. It was as if his heart was encased in ice. Though they had ceased when he discovered what was held in Blackmane's chest, the whispers had slowly returned in a low din, and he couldn't seem to shake them off.

Vol, tote, nuin mar. Vol, tote, nuin mar.

"Veran?" Teyla asked softly.

"I need some food." He stood and went up to the bar, struggling to ignore the foreboding shadow that hung over his heart.

CHAPTER SEVEN

THAT EVENING, VERAN, Teyla, Mirius, and Ruald found a spot in the woods a little ways from The Ghostly Damsel. The red sky deepened into violet as the sun set, and Veran stared up at the blushing paint strokes of clouds that covered the vast expanse. In his hand was a burlap sack, a round bulge hanging at the bottom of it.

"Will you finally show us what was in that chest?" Mirius asked, leaning against an oak and fingering his bow. "I trusted you back at the waterfall when you said we couldn't give the thing back to the guard, but I'd at least like to know why we didn't give it up. The curiosity is about to kill me."

Ruald looked perplexed. "There was something in that chest? You lied to the guard?" He looked at Teyla. "I didn't think you ever lied."

Teyla's eyes were cold. "I didn't tell a lie. I never said anything about the chest."

"You didn't volunteer any information. That's just as bad."

Teyla ignored the statement. "Veran seemed to believe that whatever was in that chest of Blackmane's shouldn't be returned to the guard. I followed his judgment."

"Well?" The dwarf huffed looking at the vampire hunter. "What was in the chest, eh?"

Veran stared at the ground, lost in thought. He opened the sack and turned it over. A yellowed skull fell out, tumbling onto the grass and landing so its hollow eyes looked up at the ruddy sky. It had sharp, lethal fangs, and carved on its forehead was a mark, a magical rune that Veran was all too familiar with.

"What is that?" Mirius asked.

"A thing of evil," Teyla breathed, her face going pale. "I recognize that mark. It's a rune used in Abyssal Magic to create links with spirits. Placed upon a part of a person's body it can recall the soul from the dead to fill the object and completely regenerate the body to its former glory. Even the etching of the rune on a toe bone would be enough."

Veran nodded. "And that particular rune, known as Nuin Mar, is marked on one of the worst vampires ever known to man. Kurnval."

Ruald looked from the skull to Veran. "Never heard of him."

"Oh, the elves have," Mirius said, his facetious demeanor now gone. "He was one of the leaders in the first war between the vampires and the únae when the tahu still dwelled in Glomora. He killed thousands upon thousands of innocents. Not exactly someone you'd want to invite to dinner... Not unless you wanted to be dinner."

"Why would Blackmane have such a thing?" Teyla asked.

"I don't know," Veran said. "But Gaika knew he had it, and she stole it from him. She was no doubt going to use it, although it would seem she didn't have the magical skill to harness its power. It's a good thing that fate sent us to intercede and get the skull back, or who knows what would have happened." He turned his attention to Ruald. "As you can imagine, I was not comfortable giving this to the guards. They would not have understood its power, and it would not have been safe with them."

Ruald stroked his beard in thought. "And you're sure you do? How do you know that's even this Kurnval and not some other vampire?"

"I was a vampire, once," Veran said. "I know much of the foul race's lore, and I'm fully aware of what kind of evil would be released from this thing if it fell into the wrong hands."

Ruald nodded. "I'm sorry. I too often forget. But what will you do with the skull now?"

The voice that had been itching in Verna's consciousness all day suddenly became louder. Its deep, icy voice echoed in his brain sending shivers about his body. He wanted to take the skull, and he wanted to use it. He wanted to return Kurnval and release his evil back into the world. He wanted to see blood staining every inch of the earth.

Vol, tote, nuin mar. Vol, tote, nuin mar.

"Veran?"

He came back to himself. Teyla's warm, soft hand was on his arm, her eyes fixed on him with concern. The sight of her eyes calmed him, and the voice in his head fell to a soft murmur.

"I'm alright." He squeezed her hand reassuringly and removed it from his arm. "I want to destroy it, but this rune also protects the object on which it is etched. Normal means, even magic, won't work."

"Then what can we do?" Mirius asked.

"We need to protect it," Teyla said. "We should take it to the Pinnacle of High Magic in Aurma. There it will be guarded from those who would use it, and the wizards there can find a way to destroy it."

Veran nodded. "I think that would be best. We can't let such an evil artifact fall into the wrong hands as it almost has already. We will collect the gold from the city guard when Parner returns, then we can set out for the Sun Court."

Teyla considered him for a moment but then a small smile graced her lips. "This will be enjoyable. I miss our old adventuring party."

"I do as well!" Ruald said vigorously. "And you lot owe me an adventure or two for missing out on this one! I will never be left behind to 'sort business' again!"

The others laughed, and as they did so, Veran felt a lightness in his heart that he hadn't felt in months. He had been traveling alone for so long, and by the grace of the gods or by the fortunate hand of fate, he had been reunited with his friends. It was not a situation he thought would be possible, but here it was coming to pass.

This is what is meant to be.

Veran jumped at the voice, soft and feminine. He looked around, but Teyla was pulling teasingly at Ruald's beard while the dwarf shouted indignantly. Mirius was in on the fun, yanking the dwarf's ears.

Naivya?

Yes, Veran, the voice responded. *I am still with you.*

A warm tingling crawled up his veins, a gentle peace entering his being.

"Thank you," he whispered.

Teyla released Ruald's beard and turned to Veran. "Shall we return to the tavern?"

He smiled. "Let's."

***

"NOT WANTING TO join in the revels?" Mirius sat down on the bench next to Veran.

They were outside of The Ghostly Damsel, and music and laughter could be heard from behind the wooden walls of the tavern. It was a fine autumn night, with clear, bejeweled skies and a moon with a lopsided smile.

"Just wanted some quiet." Veran had a tankard he was sipping from, enjoying the same cinnamon ale that Sonja had served him the night before. The dark chanting had faded from his mind since Naivya had spoken to him in the forest, and for the first time in a long while, he felt a soothing calm.

"Another fine adventure, we've had, eh?" Mirius said. "Bandits, vampires, gold. Too bad I'm not a poet, or I'd write some verse about it."

"You're as talented a poet as I am an archer," Veran said with a smirk.

Mirius chuckled. "Well, none of us are perfect, are we? Take Ruald, for example. Now there's a fine specimen of a bard. He's so drunk from ale that he's telling that Sonja girl inside that he'd whisk her away and shower her in jewels and rich snake furs."

Veran laughed. "What an idiot."

"Agreed. Teyla is trying to pry him away from the poor girl as we speak."

The two friends watched the skies in silence. Mirius softly hummed a melody that Veran recognized as being popular among the musicians of the Moon Court. A breeze rustled the trees, sending dried, crisp leaves twirling to the grass.

"Did you and Teyla talk?" the elf asked. "While I was searching the cave?"

Veran nodded. "That we did. And we still don't see eye to eye on my magic."

Mirius sighed. "Veran, you might want to listen to her. She knows a thing or two about magic. Remember, that's why you and I sought her out in the first place all those years ago when we looked into those mysterious deaths. She was also once a member of the Council of the Pinnacle of High Magic, don't forget."

Veran said nothing. Deep down, he knew that Teyla had a point about his magic. But she didn't understand. It was too much a part of him for him to ignore. Still…

He looked at ShadowWeep, which rested against the wall next to him. The sword's jewels glimmered like the stars above him. Watching him, staring into him. The sword was his past, present, and future, and the magic that it gave him was also a piece of him. The blade was woven into the very fabric of his soul.

He turned his attention back to the night, to its mixture of shadows and lights. "What concerns me more right now, Mirius, is that a lone vampire had the skull of Kurnval. It concerns me that Blackmane had it as well."

"Perhaps Blackmane just thought it was some sort of artifact? Something for his collection?" Mirius stretched out his legs and rested his arms behind his head. "I think you're thinking too much into it. I think that vampire whore was just using it for her own gain. Or maybe it was just plain dumb luck that she stumbled upon it."

Veran wasn't so sure. But he was glad that the skull would be safe and that no harm would come from it or Gaika. As much as he wished that she would have taken his offer of redemption, he knew he had done his duty in killing her. And as they would set out for the Sun Court soon, he hoped he would continue to succeed in his mission of redeeming himself.

"Teyla also told me about her visions," Veran said.

"Oh?"

"What do you think of them?"

"I think that my knowledge of magic is limited," Mirius said. "And I think that these visions that Teyla has been having are a precursor to many adventures to come. And adventure, as we both know, is always an opportunity for gold."

Veran cracked a smile. "You have a very one-track mind."

The elf shrugged. "I know what I want. That's not

such a bad thing."

Veran continued smiling, then stood. "Come on, my friend. This may be one of the last nights we get to sleep under a roof for some time."

Mirius grinned and leaped up. "Sounds excellent. Let's also see if we can help Teyla get our short, bald friend away from that innocent beauty you scared half to death today."

They both entered the tavern to its warm light and to Ruald 's boorish claims that he would kill a thousand, nay, a million snakes if he could but have the hand of the lovely barmaid of The Ghostly Damsel. Veran laughed with the rest of the patrons of the tavern. He was ready for a good night's sleep, and after that, the road ahead.

ACKNOWLEDGEMENTS

I want to start off by thanking my mom for teaching me to love reading at a young age. And I want to thank my dad for never dissuading my weirdness, even if I constantly "thought I was an elf." Y'all's love and support mean the world to me.

To Ariel Paiement, aka Abigail Corder (my editor/wife). Your encouragement and the answers to my constant questions about publishing were invaluable. I couldn't have done it without you.

I want to thank Caleb and Petra Everson, Elizabeth Craig, Erin Peck, Rebekah Sanders, and Aly Corder for beta-reading this book. Your suggestions were invaluable.

Thanks to Jonathan Hoyle, Elizabeth Craig, Erin Peck, and Wil Wright for allowing me to express this story through my very first *Dungeons and Dragons* game. You allowing me to express my ideas paved the way for them to make it onto the pages of a book.

Thanks to Jonathan Vickery and *The People Sentinel* for giving me the opportunity to write a weekly literary column and share my love for stories with the residents of Barnwell County.

Thank you to Edward Wald and Bob Snead at the Palmetto Innovation Center for helping me design a decent author's website. Y'all are wizards of technology!

Thanks to everyone in the Barnwell County Consolidated School District in the Williston schools who in one way or another supported my craft.

And finally, thanks be to my Lord and Savior, Jesus Christ. You gave me the ability to write and to tell stories, and I offer this book as Worship to You.

48

ABOUT THE AUTHOR

David B. Corder lives in South Carolina where he teaches middle school English Language Arts. He also writes for his local paper, *The People Sentinel*. He lives in a house crammed with books; action figures; one old, yet energetic, border collie named Izzy; a tyrant of a pit bull named Guinevere; and his wife and fellow author, Ariel Paiement.

David has other hobbies when he's not writing. He likes to play heavy metal guitar, games like *Dungeons and Dragons* and *Magic: The Gathering*, and video games. And naturally, he reads because you can't be a writer without reading lots of books. He also used to make a practice of ignoring the dirty dishes that piled up in his sink, but married life has taught him that that isn't a good idea.

You can find David on the web at davidbcorder.com or contact him at dbcorderwriter@gmail.com.

Enjoyed this book?

Leave a Review on Amazon

Follow David at:
Web: davidbcorder.com
Email: dbcorderwriter@gmail.com
Substack: davidbcorder.substack.com
Amazon: www.amazon.com/stores/David-B.-
Corder/author/B0D46882R6

Did you enjoy this story and want to continue reading about the Realms of Glomora? Get free short stories and more in your inbox by signing up for David's newsletter. Go to davidbcorder.com and sign up today!

Made in the USA
Columbia, SC
16 August 2024

39994501R00030